This book belongs to:
. . . .
D1261688

Contents

Peppa's
arty."

The children decide to make their own circus.
"We can call it Peppa's Circus!" says Peppa.

Granny Pig thinks this is a splendid idea.
She fetches the dressing-up box.

There are lots of good circus costumes in the dressing-up box.

Peppa finds a top hat. Danny Dog finds some spotty trunks and a stick-on moustache.

"I want to be a clown!" cries Peppa.

Too late. Pedro Pony has already put on the clown outfit. Rebecca Rabbit does his clown make-up.

Everybody has a job except Peppa.

"Peppa can be the ringmaster," says Grandpa Pig.
"The ringmaster is the boss!"
"Yes!" nods Peppa. "I can be the ringmaster."

The garden party guests arrive. Granny Pig shows them into the tent.

"Ladies and gentlemen," cries Peppa. "Welcome to my circus!"

"Now," says Peppa. "Please be very scared of the amazing Candy Cat!"
Rebecca Rabbit holds out a hoop for Candy Cat to jump through.

George, Richard and Edmond come out next.

They ride round and
round on their tricycles.

"Don't stop clapping," calls Peppa.
"Here's the strong Danny Dog!"

Danny lifts Peppa high up into the air.

The crowd goes wild. Danny Dog is very strong.

Ummph!

Now it is Emily Elephant's turn. She juggles two potatoes and an egg.

"Oooooh!" gasps the audience.

It is the end of Peppa's amazing circus. "That," Granny Pig laughs, "is the best circus I have ever seen!"

The Children's Fête

Peppa and her friends are at playgroup. Mr Bull is checking the school roof.

"Moo!" shouts Mr Bull. "Who put this roof on for you?"
"You did, Mr Bull," says Madame Gazelle.
Mr Bull nods. "Lovely job! It will last you a lifetime."

Madame Gazelle takes Mr Bull inside.
She points to the ceiling. It is leaking water.
"Look!" she says. "It is going drip-drip!"

"You need a new roof," says Mr Bull.

"Where are we going to get the money for a new school roof?" asks Madame Gazelle.

The children have a good idea. They decide to put on a school fête to get the money for the new school roof.

It is the day of the children's fête. Danny Dog is in charge of the microphone.
"Hello, grown-ups!" he says.
"Get your money out for the new school roof!"

Emily Elephant is in charge
of the bric-a-brac stall.
"Roll up, roll up," she calls.
"All sorts of bits and bobs!"

"Hmm . . ." says Mr Fox. "This all looks very interesting."
Mr Fox is always looking for bric-a-brac.

"Balloons!" shouts Pedro Pony.
"Lovely balloons!"
"May I have a red one?"
says Madame Gazelle.
"How much money have you
got?" asks Pedro.
Madame Gazelle tips all of
the coins out of her purse.

Clink!

Suzy Sheep is in charge of the face-painting stall.

"Can I be a mountain leopard please?" says Miss Rabbit.

"No," says Suzy. "I can only do fruit."

"OK," says Miss Rabbit.
"Can I be . . ."
"A plum!" decides Suzy.

Mr Bull comes to visit Peppa.
He has got a green face.
"I am an apple!" he booms.

"Would you like to try the lucky dip?" asks Peppa.
"Everyone's a winner!"

Mr Bull drops
a coin into
Peppa's tin.

Mr Bull reaches into
the lucky dip barrel. He pulls out a dolly.
"Can I have a go?" asks Mrs Cat.
Mrs Cat wins a toy digger.

"Oh!" gasps Peppa. "Do you want to swap?"
Mr Bull and Mrs Cat do not want to swap.

They are pleased with their lucky dip prizes!

Pant!
Puff!

Freddy Fox calls all the grown-ups. It is time for the mummies and daddies race. Everybody has to get into a sack and jump across the field.

"On your marks, get set . . . GO!" shouts Freddy.

The mummies and daddies have lots of fun jumping in sacks. At the end, Madame Gazelle has an important announcement to make.

"We have raised enough money to buy a new school roof!" she cries. "Again!"

Granny Pig's Perfume

Squirt!

Peppa and George are visiting Granny and Grandpa's house. Peppa is watching Granny Pig at her dressing table.
"You smell nice, Granny!" says Peppa.
"Thank you," says Granny Pig. "It's my perfume de lavender."

Granny Pig's perfume smells
like her garden.
"Perfume is made of flowers,"
Granny Pig tells Peppa.

Peppa asks for a glass of water.
"Now I'm going to put flowers in
it and make perfume," she says.

George comes to see what
Peppa is doing in the garden.
"I'm making perfume," she says.
"It's going to be the prettiest,
smelliest perfume ever!"

"Snort!"
George wants to watch
Peppa making perfume.

"First I pick a smelly flower," says Peppa, "then I put it in my beaker."

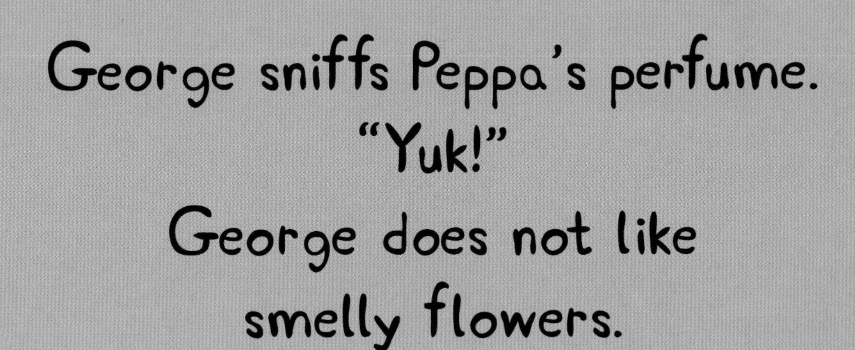

George sniffs Peppa's perfume.
"Yuk!"
George does not like
smelly flowers.

Grandpa Pig is in his herb garden.
"Smell this!" says Peppa.
"Poo-ey!" snorts Grandpa Pig.
"It smells like pond water."

Peppa explains that the smell is her special perfume. Grandpa takes another sniff. "Oh yes!" he decides. "It is the most beautiful perfume in the world!"

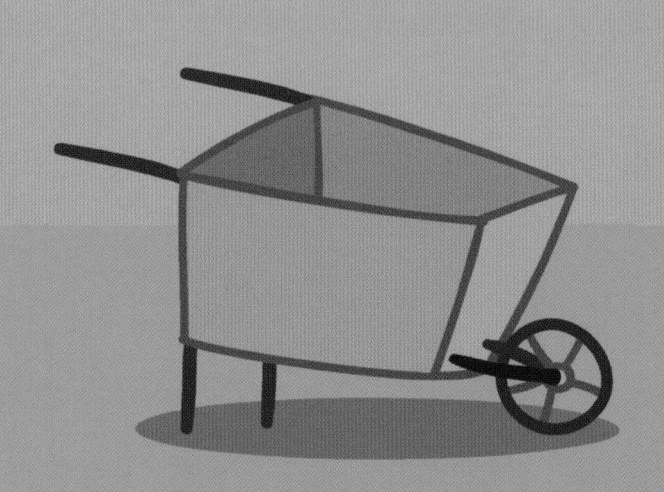

George still does not like Peppa's flower perfume.
"Take this bucket," says Grandpa Pig.
"You can make perfume out of something else."
There are lots of lovely smelly things in Grandpa Pig's herb garden.

"This is rosemary," says Grandpa Pig. "I like to use it in my cooking."

"Hmm . . ." sniffs Peppa.
"It smells interesting."
"Eugh!" splutters George.

George still hasn't made any perfume. He doesn't like the smell of anything. "There must be something that you like the smell of?" says Grandpa Pig.

George goes off to find a muddy puddle.
He fills up his bucket.

George runs back.
He gives the bucket to
Granny Pig to sniff.

"Actually," she says,
"that smells quite nice."
"It smells lovely!"
agrees Peppa.

Grandpa Pig sniffs George's bucket. "I say!" he snorts. "That is delightful!"

"What did you put in the perfume, George?" asks Grandpa Pig.

George runs back to the muddy puddle. "George's perfume is made out of muddy puddles!" giggles Peppa. "Aah!" says Granny Pig. "Perfume de muddy puddle!"

Sniff!
Sniff!

Peppa, George, Granny Pig and Grandpa Pig all jump in the muddy puddle.

"Granny Pig!" snorts Peppa. "You smell even nicer than you did before!"

Grandpa Pig agrees. Maybe Granny Pig should wear perfume de muddy puddle more often!

Peppa's Sandpit

Peppa and her friends are playing in the sandpit.

"This sandpit is our desert island!" decides Peppa. "We will live here forever."
"If we are going to live here forever I want it to be nice," says Suzy Sheep.

"The desert island just needs some houses," says Peppa.
"And roads!" barks Danny Dog.
"And shops!" says Suzy Sheep.

"Dine-saw!" shout George and Richard.
"Yes!" snorts Peppa. "The desert island can have dinosaurs, too!"

Emily Elephant looks at the desert island.
She thinks that it needs trees.
"Where are we going to get trees from?"
asks Suzy.

Danny Dog has an idea. "We have to drive big trucks around the world and look for trees!"

The dinosaurs guard the desert island while the others go to find some trees.

"Hello Mummy Rabbit," says Danny. "Have you got any spare trees?" Mummy Rabbit picks up some sticks. "There you go!"

Peppa and her friends drive their trucks back around the world. They plant the trees.

"There," says Peppa.

"We will live here forever!"

Candy Cat and Zoe Zebra come to see the desert island. "It would be really good if it had a lake," says Candy.

Danny digs a lake. Now it needs some water. The children pretend to fly around the world looking for water.

Pedro Pony is playing on the roundabout.
"I know where there is pretend snow," he says.
"We can melt it to get pretend water!"

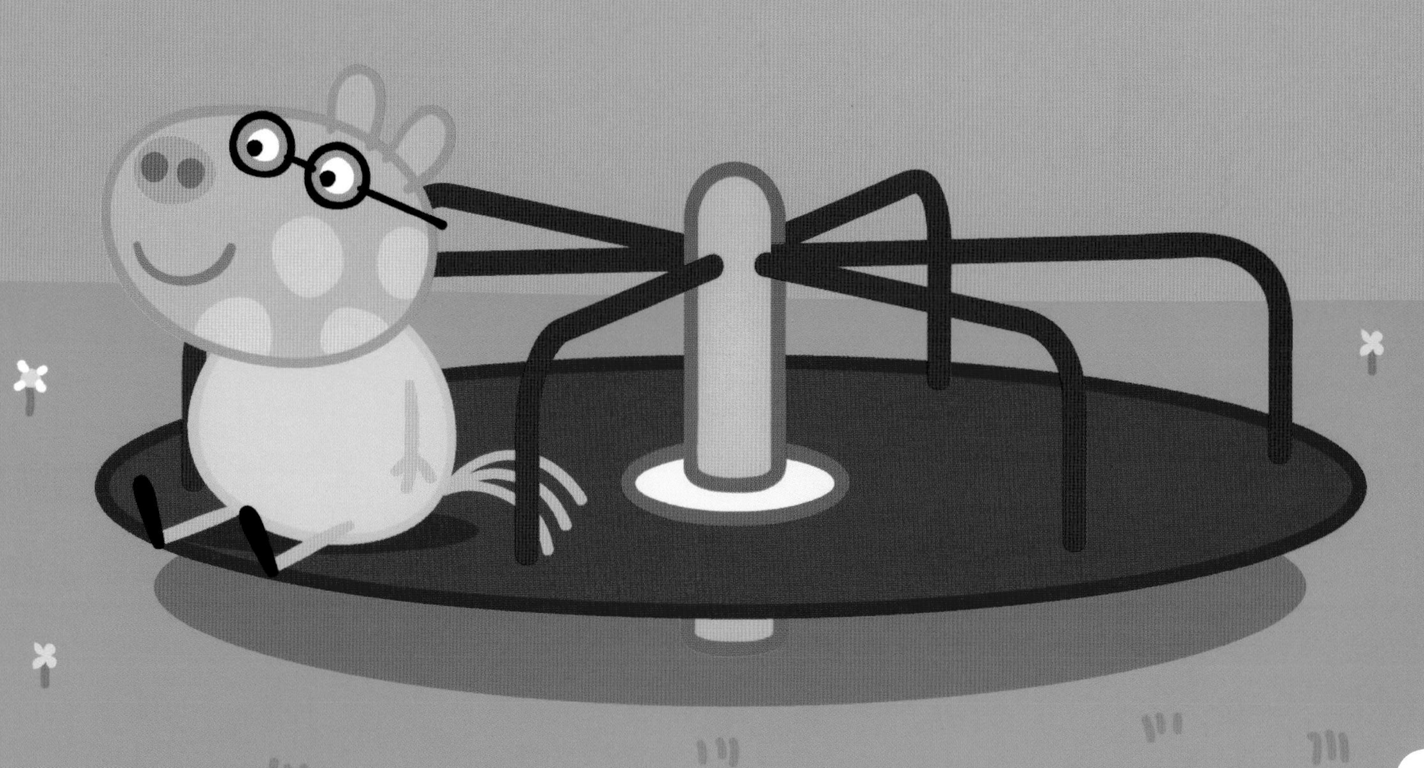

"This is a pretend mountain!" shouts Pedro.

Pedro climbs to the top of the mountain,
but there is no snow up there.
It has melted in the sun.
"Can't we pretend that it hasn't melted?"
says Suzy.
"No," neighs Pedro. "It has melted good
and proper."

Candy spots Daddy Pig. He is drinking from the water fountain.

"Can we have some water in our bucket please?" asks Peppa.

"Ho ho!" snorts Daddy Pig. "Of course."

Tee! Hee! Hee!

The children fly back to the desert island.
Peppa fills up the lake.

"We've got water!" giggles Peppa.

Freddy Fox arrives. The desert island
is nearly ready.
"If only it had some flags," sighs Zoe.

Mr Fox takes a look in his van.
He has got everything in his van.
"How about these?" he grins.

Est. 2010
Yay!

Now the desert island is perfect. It has trees, roads, shops, dinosaurs, flags and a real lake.

"We can live here forever and ever!" cheers Peppa.

Grampy Rabbit in Space

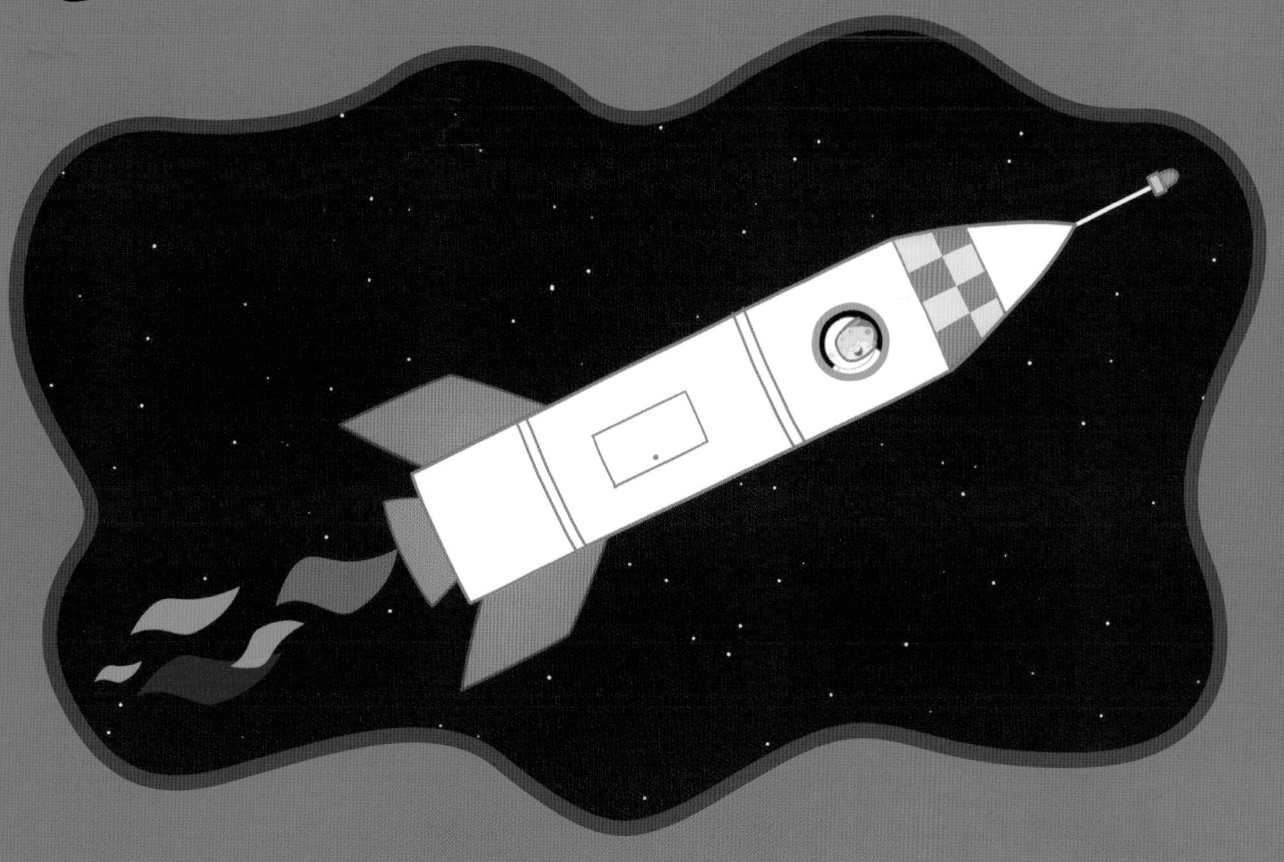

Peppa and her friends are at playgroup.
Today they have a special treat.
Grampy Rabbit is here to talk
about space rockets!

"Wocket!"
snorts George.
"Brrmm!"

"Hello, everybody!"
Grampy Rabbit shouts.
Grampy Rabbit
has a very
loud voice.

He holds up a
space rocket.
"It's a bit small!"
says Suzy Sheep.
"This is just a
model," explains
Grampy Rabbit.

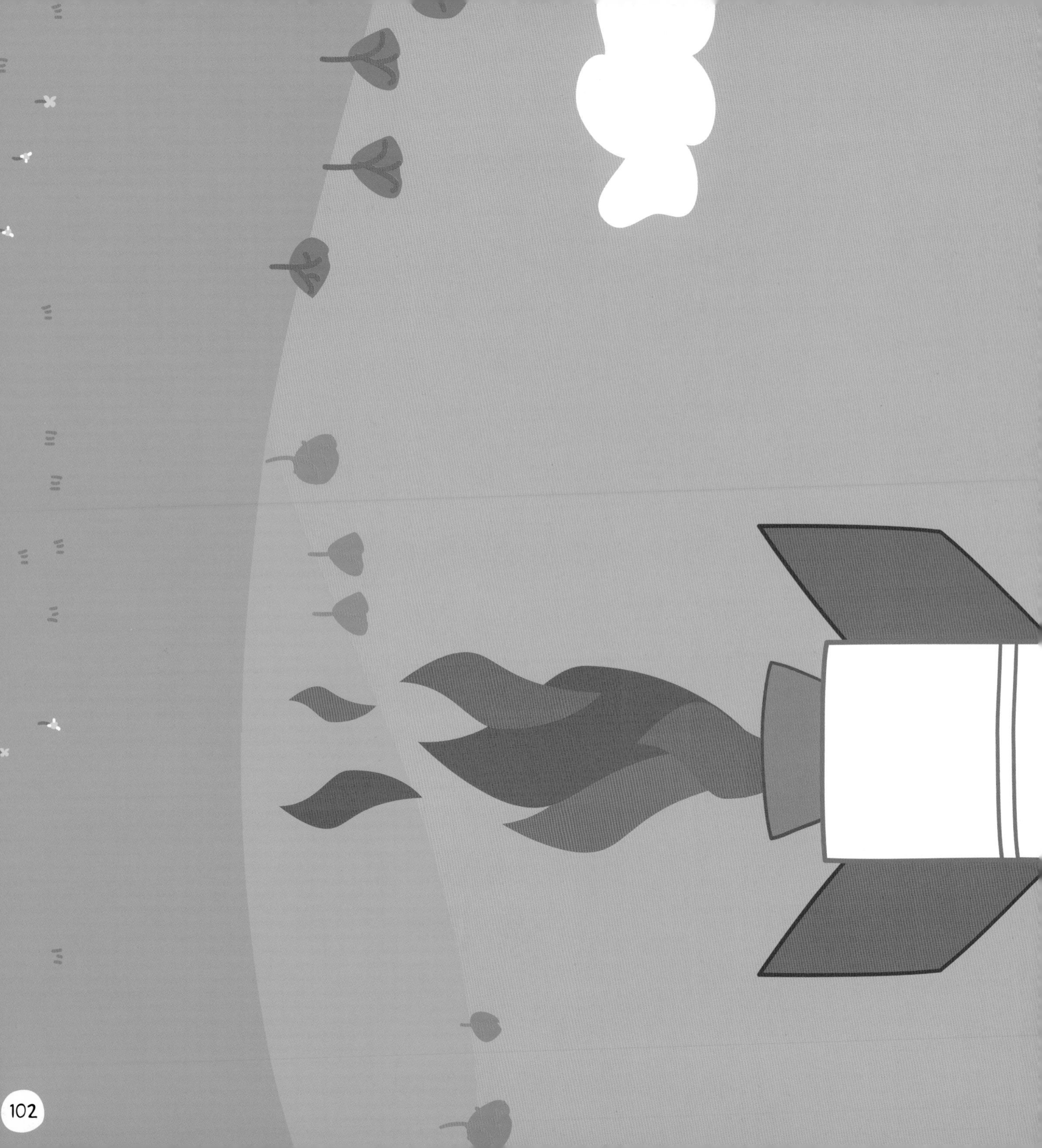

"The rocket I went in
was ginormous!"

Everyone gasps.
Grampy Rabbit has
flown to the
moon in a space rocket!

Grampy Rabbit lifts the rocket into the air. "When you go into space, you count backwards," he says. "Five, four, three, two, one . . . BLAST OFF!"

Peppa and her friends all shout together. "BLAST OFF!"

"There I was, flying through space,"
remembers Grampy Pig.
"Ooh!" say the children.

VRROOOM!

"When I landed on the moon," says Grampy Rabbit, "it was so beautiful I was lost for words."

"That sounds nice," sighs Madame Gazelle.

Grampy Rabbit goes on. "Did you know that when you're on the moon you can jump as high as a house?"

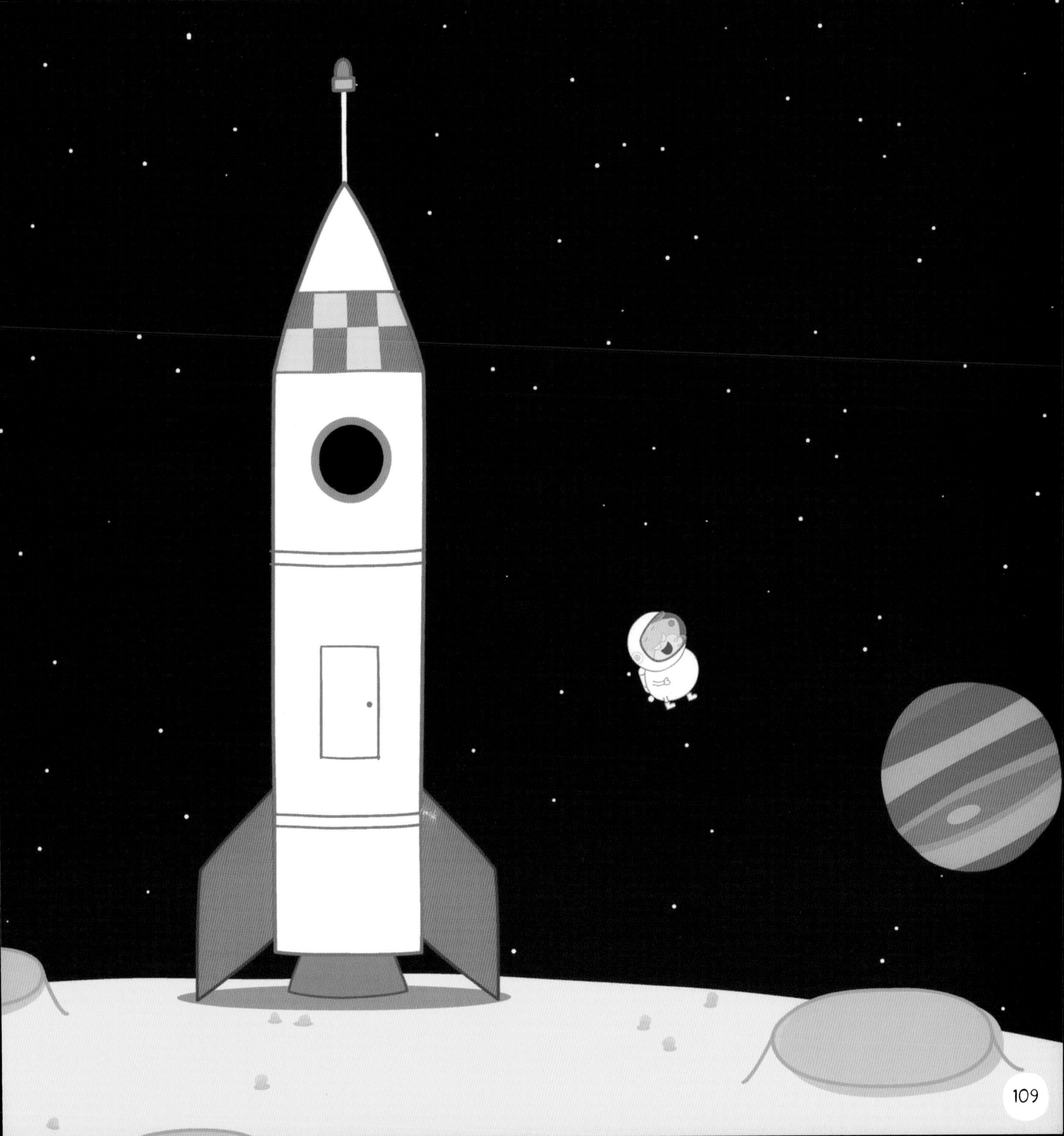

Suddenly something strange happens.
Grampy Rabbit stops talking!

"Oh dear," says Madame Gazelle. "He has lost his voice."
Madame Gazelle asks Doctor Brown Bear to come
and help Grampy Rabbit.

Doctor Brown Bear looks into Grampy Rabbit's mouth. "I see," he says. "A very serious case of losing a voice."

The doctor pours some special pink medicine on to his spoon. "Open wide!" he says.

Grampy Rabbit swallows the medicine.

"Try saying 'ahh' now," says Doctor Brown Bear. The doctor listens carefully.

"AAAAHHHHHHHH!" booms Grampy Rabbit. The medicine has made his voice much better!

Grampy Rabbit gets back to his story.

"I wrote a song on the moon," he cries. "Would you like to hear it?"
"No, thank you," say Madame Gazelle and Doctor Brown Bear.
"Yes, please!" say the children.

Twang!

"All together now . . ." sings Grampy Rabbit.

"I got up this morning,
I went to the moon,
And all I could see,
Was the moon and the stars!
The moon, the stars,
the moon, the stars,
the moon, the stars!"

Everybody loves
singing along with
Grampy Rabbit.

Mr Bull in a China Shop

It's a lovely day. Daddy Pig is taking everyone out for a drive.
"Stop!" shouts Mr Bull.
"We're digging up the road."

"Digger!" shouts George.
George likes diggers.

Daddy Pig waits at the red light.
"Will the digging take long?"
asks Mummy Pig.

"It will take as long as it takes!" shouts Mr Bull.
Mr Bull walks off. It is time for his tea break.

"Oh dear. Now we'll have to wait even longer," says Mummy Pig.

"Why don't you join us?" booms Mr Bull.

"Thank you!" Mummy Pig smiles.
Everybody sits down.
Mr Bull pours out the tea.

"That's a nice teapot,"
says Peppa.
"Yes!" snorts Mr Bull.
"It's made of
delicate china."

Mr Bull puts
the teapot
down on the
table too hard.
"Oh no," he yells.
"I've broken it!"

Mr Bull doesn't know his own strength sometimes. He is very sad.

"Miss Rabbit has a china shop," says Mummy Pig. "She could mend the teapot."

"Good idea!" shouts Mr Bull. "We'll go right now!"

Mr Bull drives all the way to the china shop. Miss Rabbit is hard at work. "Moo!" bellows Mr Bull.

Miss Rabbit looks up. "Aaagh!" she wails. "A bull in a china shop!"

000

"I have broken my china teapot!" cries Mr Bull.
Miss Rabbit takes a look at the teapot.

"Hmm," she frowns.
"That's very broken . . . but
I think I can fix it."

Miss Rabbit gets out some glue. Fixing a teapot is like doing a jigsaw puzzle.
"The pieces fit together," says Peppa.
"There's just one funny-shaped bit left," says Miss Rabbit.
Peppa giggles. Miss Rabbit has found the handle!

Miss Rabbit gives the
teapot back to Mr Bull.
"It's as good as new!"
he bellows. "Thank you."

"Be careful not to smash
it again," says
Miss Rabbit.
"I am very good at
smashing things!"
agrees Mr Bull.

Ho! Ho!
000

Outside the china shop there is a hole in the road. "Look, boss," says Mr Labrador.

Mr Bull makes up his mind. Miss Rabbit can't have a hole outside her shop!

"You fixed my teapot," shouts Mr Bull. "I'll fix your road!"

"How are you going to mend the hole?" wonders Peppa.

Mr Bull grins.
"We'll dig up
the road!"
Mr Bull likes digging
up the road!